Gun

Ray Banks

CRIME EXPRESS

Gun
by Ray Banks

Published by Crime Express in 2008
Crime Express is an imprint of
Five Leaves Publications,
PO Box 8786, Nottingham NG1 9AW
www.fiveleaves.co.uk

ISBN: 978 1905512 522

Crime Express 7

Five Leaves acknowledges financial support
from Arts Council England

ARTS COUNCIL ENGLAND

Five Leaves is a member of Inpress
www.inpressbooks.co.uk),
representing independent publishers

Typesetting and design:
Four Sheets Design and Print
Printed in Great Britain

1

'Course, when he thought back on it, it was all Goose's fault. He was the one gave him the job in the first place.

"You want to know what a real war is, you have to go right back to the last big one, the last World War. There, right, you was looking at total annihilation of a democratic way of life. Fuck the rest of them." Goose started counting on his fingers. "Korea? Police action. Vietnam? Police action. The Falklands?"

Goose paused, sucked his teeth. Then looked at the lad in front of him.

"Last ditch attempt to curry favour with the general public by sending us all out there to slaughter a bunch of fuckin' shepherds. Don't get us wrong about it or nowt. I was over there, I did what I had to do. And I wasn't under any fuckin' illusions about it, neither. I mean, I knew we was the better soldiers, we was the *trained* ones. Them lads, the only things they was supposed to be good at was shearing and dying. But them cunts managed to get lucky a couple times." He slapped his stump. "Including the time they took me leg off us, the bastards."

Goose fell silent. Looked like he was waiting for Richie to say something. Behind Goose's wheelchair, BBC News 24 rattled on slightly.

And Richie didn't want to get into it. Wasn't even fucking born when Goose was over there. Didn't know what to say.

So he said, "Right y'are."

Goose's eyes dropped to slits, then he ducked to the tray in front of him, snorted a thick line of coke. When he came back, he thumbed one nostril. Pointed at Richie. "You just got out?"

"Aye."

"How long?"

"Give us eighteen month, like."

"A fuckin' tickle," said Goose. "What for?"

Richie frowned. "You told us to go round and chin Hacky Curtis, remember?"

Goose started to shake his head until something fired in his brain. "Oh, aye. Right, I thought that was a kid I told to do that."

Richie looked at the carpet. "Aye."

"How old?"

"Sixteen, almost seventeen."

"And they got you on GBH, did they?"

"Nah, it was Actual," said Richie.

"Right, then you didn't do what I told you to do, did you?"

Richie looked up, his mouth open.

"I say chin someone," said Goose, "you get a GBH."

"He was in the hospital. And I was at Deerbolt."

"That's for adults, son."

"I got in trouble at the remand."

Goose regarded the lad. "You know, you get caught again, that's it."

Richie nodded.

"That's you right back in the shit, back at the

YOI."

"Aye," said Richie. "They explained it to us. But then I could go back to the shit just being here with you. Known criminal an' that." He wiped his nose, smiled. "Jumped the Metty to get here an' all."

"What d'you want, a fuckin' badge?"

"Nah, I want a job."

Goose blinked at Richie. Then he burst out laughing. It was a low sound, cackling high in the middle. A coke laugh that tore right through Richie, tensed him up. Goose shook his head, waved one hand at him.

"Wex said you had jobs going, like," said Richie.

"Oh, Wex, is it?"

Goose's laugh wound down to a chuckle. He ran his tongue over his bottom teeth, then breathed out. Kept glancing at Richie with this weird smile on his face. A lot of thoughts running through Richie's head, the same old story about a lost leg on Goose Green when everyone knew what really happened — stupid bastard mainlined an artery. But you never said that to

Goose. He might've been a fucking cripple and nose-deep in his own product, but Goose had a rep that stretched back since before the riots. And that rep was what brought Richie over today.

"Wex," said Goose again, and there wasn't any laughter in his voice now. "That twat wants a fuckin' seeing-to, he keeps sending people round here. I got dealers, son. And I got muscle. So unless you want to run errands —"

"Okay," said Richie.

Goose smiled. "You got a family to support?"

Richie thought about lying. Realised that Goose probably already knew about his girl-friend. Even if he didn't, it wasn't so hard to find out. "Aye."

Goose nodded, as if that was the answer he was hoping for. He shifted his arse in the wheel-chair. "I got something, maybe. Not much, like. But it'll pay."

"Alright."

"You keep this to yourself."

"You can trust us."

"I know I can, else I wouldn't be telling you."

His eyes narrowed. "I need protection."

Richie didn't say anything.

"You know what I'm talking about," said Goose.

"Aye. And I thought you had a gun."

Goose looked long and hard at Richie, one eye going lazy. "I had one, aye. But now I need another one." He grinned wide. "You can never have too many fuckin' guns around the place, the job I'm in. And it's not like I'm going to give anyone a good kicking, is it?"

Richie smiled, but he didn't laugh. He knew better than to laugh in Goose's presence. A smile you could explain away if the cripple got bolshy; laughter was a lot harder, and if Goose reckoned you were laughing at *him*, you could forget about it. He'd been know to launch himself at blokes, especially if he'd had a couple of lines before the meeting. And right then, Richie was glad Goose didn't have a gun, because the man's eyes narrowed, waiting for the smile to turn into a laugh.

"What d'you want us to do?" said Richie.

Goose moved again in his wheelchair. The

coke made him itchy, and Richie had to drop his eyes whenever he moved his stump. Then Goose breathed out hard as he dropped back into his seat. In his hand was a stack of cash, all fivers. He tossed it to Richie. The money was still arse warm.

"You know the Leam?"

Richie nodded. "Been there a couple times."

"So you know how to get there and back in a day."

"Not that far, is it?"

"I know it's not. I'm wondering if *you* know. So's I don't get the fuckin' excuses later on that you didn't know where you was going and now you're fuckin' lost."

"I'm not like that." Richie raised his chin. "I been down there, I can handle it."

"Alright then. There's a gadgie on the Leam called Florida Al. I'll write down the address." He pulled out a small pen, wrote the address on a used bus ticket he'd found in his pocket. Handed it to Richie — a house number and address. Richie had an idea where it was. Wasn't that far from the Metro station, so he could probably walk it.

When Richie looked up, Goose had a mobile phone in his hands.

"What's that for?"

"In case you get any bother."

"I won't."

Goose raised his eyebrows. "Like fuck, you won't. I know Al, and I know what kind of fuckin' gyppo the bastard can be. Anyone goes there on my behalf, he's going to try and skin you. Cunt thinks he's fuckin' special. But we all know he's not, and the fuckin' Jocks know he's not an' all. Lad couldn't even run a stand-and-tan, he's hardly the fuckin' Godfather. Anyway, you think he's trying something on, he gives you any shit, you give us a ring on that — the number's in the contacts — and you put him on the fuckin' line. I'll straighten him out."

He barked a laugh, handed Richie the phone, who felt weighed down with all this stuff.

"He asks you what gun you've come to pick up, it's a Brocock ME38 Magnum, right? Al should've already procured and drilled the fucker. He should've loaded it an' all." Goose pointed. "You better check on that an' all, because he'll fuck us out of bullets if he thinks he'll get away with it."

"Okay."

"Either way, you get the gun, you give us a ring."

"Got you," said Richie. He straightened his hoodie, tried to pat the pockets flat, then made to leave.

"One last thing," said Goose.

Richie nodded.

"You know who I am."

"Aye."

"So you know what happens to people with notions."

Richie breathed out. Slowly, so Goose wouldn't notice. He knew what happened. He wasn't daft. Them lads down in Gateshead, that ginger dealer called Moses and his mate. Goose sent down a couple of smackheads with a hunger to take their fucking teeth out. That was the rumour anyway. And Richie wasn't about to question it.

2

Richie got the Metro through to town, then changed at Monument and headed south. When he got to Heworth, he checked his watch. He was supposed to go down the dole today, but this job from Goose meant it'd probably have to wait until tomorrow. His Becka would be disappointed, but that'd have to be the way it was. He couldn't make money and look for a job at the same time. She'd understand. She'd have to. It was the way he always provided.

"You're a skivvy," she said to him once she'd had a skinful. "You do that running around for these people like you're their fuckin' slave. If you was a smackhead, I could understand, y'know, you'd be *itching* about something. But you're not. And you still do it."

"It's a job."

"It's something that's gonna fuckin' *kill* you one of these days." And she'd get tearful, wave her hand and leave the room before he got a chance to calm her down.

Then he'd be sat there, staring at the telly, a can of Ace going warm in his hand. Thinking she was right, but there wasn't nothing he could do about it. A man had to work, and he made better money taking care of things for Goose than he ever did in a job-type job.

Still, it bugged fuck out of him that Goose didn't remember Hacky Curtis. Richie went to remand because of that twat, and it was all down to Goose that he did the fucking time. See, when the polis came round, knocked Richie up the morning after he put the boot to Curtis, it was Goose's name they kept saying. When they brought him in, Goose was all they wanted to hear about. And just before they shoved him into the eighteen month stretch, it was the same old questions, the same old shite.

Richie hadn't said a word.

He got on the 15 that took him to Leam Lane, took about quarter of an hour. He hopped off the bus and pulled at his hoodie. It was still morning, still had that chill in the air. And this place wasn't his usual haunt. From what he knew about the Leam it was notoriously territorial. Your face didn't fit, you shouldn't be hanging round for long. That was his experience of the place, anyway.

Richie took the address out of his pocket and looked at it. He had an idea where the street was, reckoned he remembered from the last time he was down here, and headed that way. He kept one hand in his pocket, tightly gripping the bundle of money. He stopped for a moment to light a tab, then he carried on, sucking in nicotine and keeping an eye out for anyone who might fancy confrontation.

Nobody did. But that didn't stop Richie's arse from tightening right up when he saw a bloke heading down the path of Florida Al's house, staring right at him. The bloke carried himself like a bouncer gone to seed, and looked as if all this standing outside a door on an empty street had made him slap-happy.

"Fuck d'you think you're going?"

Richie pointed behind the bloke with his free hand. "In there."

"What for?"

"None of yours."

"Like fuck."

"See Al."

"Like *fuck*. You?"

"On behalf of someone."

"On behalf?" The bloke smiled, the word alien in his mouth. "Who?"

Richie didn't know if he was allowed to name-drop. He figured what the fuck. "Goose."

The doorknob looked at him for a long time after he heard that word. Richie reckoned he'd hit a nerve, jogged a memory. Maybe both.

"Alright then, son. I'll bring you in."

The bouncer led the way, opened the UPVC door a crack and shouted through, "Got one?"

"Aye," said someone from inside. "Got the call."

The bouncer nudged the door open, and Richie stepped inside the house to the smell of pizza. His gut bubbled at the thought.

"Straight up," said the bouncer.

Florida Al was in the living room, sitting in the couch like he'd fallen and couldn't get up. Next to him was a massive, quarter-eaten pizza. He wore a silk Aloha shirt that framed chilled, pale skin and clung to a spare tyre that belonged on a monster truck. Richie stood in the doorway, didn't know if he should clear his throat or something. Al seemed intent on the television.

Then Al's eyes flickered to Richie. "Who're you?"

"I'm here to pick something up for Goose."

"I didn't ask that. What's your fuckin' name?"

"Richie."

"Good."

Al struggled to sit up, nudged the pizza box with his ample thigh in the process. Richie tried not to watch. Al sucked his teeth and muted the television. Waved one hand for Richie to come further into the room. He did, and when he glanced at the telly, saw the two naked blokes going at it like dogs.

Al was watching him, with half a smug smile creating more chins. "You mind if we have this on? Or is it too distracting for you?"

"Nah, y'alright," said Richie. "Don't do nowt for me."

"So what was it you were picking up?"

Richie sniffed. Wondered why this fat poof was testing him so much. "How, look, Goose sent us, right? He told us to go pick up a Brocock ME38 Magnum, drilled and loaded."

"Right, so he's already paid for it, has he?"

Richie stared at Florida Al and shook his head. "Nah."

Al smiled wider now, revealing teeth that belonged in the middle ages. Richie was positive he could see green in there. Al moved his head slowly, and Richie caught a little movement in his peripheral. He glanced that way, saw a cracked door to what he guessed was the kitchen. There was someone in there, watching.

When he looked back at Al, there was a gun on the coffee table. Richie guessed it was the right one — certainly *looked* like a Magnum. Al jerked his chins at Richie. "Money."

Richie removed the banded notes and put them on the table next to the gun. Made a move to pick it up and got Al's thick hand on top of his, pinning him to the table. Richie tried to move, but the big lad had some strength. Still, he didn't want to be bent over in a poof's house any longer than necessary. And it was only necessary for a fraction of a second at the most.

"Leave the gun for a second. Let me count."

Richie nodded, then whipped his hand back, straightened up as soon as he could. Watched the fat fuck pull the bands off the money and count each note, his lips moving. When Al finally gave him the nod, Richie had to stop himself lunging for the gun and running out. Instead he lifted the weapon and looked at it.

"It's loaded, right?"

Al looked up from the money. "Aw, you don't trust us, do you?"

Richie shook his head. Thinking he should probably call Goose because this was just the kind of shite he was talking about. But also thinking, fuck it, he could handle one obese arse bandit. He raised the gun and pointed it directly at Al.

"Now what's that supposed to prove?" said Al.

"I can't open this thing up," said Richie. "But I can pull a fuckin' trigger nae bother."

"I get you. And you reckon you can do that before my man Stanley peppers the shite out of you from the kitchen."

The cracked kitchen door. Right enough, Richie's instincts were spot on about that. They were spot on about this, too. This gun wasn't loaded. If it was, even if Al did have Stanley in the kitchen, he'd still be thinking about his fat arse getting splattered all over that cheap sofa, so there'd still be a twitch or something.

Richie thought, fuck it, and pulled the trigger.

Click.

There was still a jump, a wave running through Al's body caused by a single tiny flinch somewhere under the Aloha. He breathed out through his nose, then he shifted around, pushed aside a cushion and brought out a small plastic bag with six bullets inside. He tossed it onto the coffee table.

"There," said Al.

Richie scooped up the bag, stuffed into his pocket. Then he slid the Magnum into the back of his trackies and smiled at Al. "Thanks."

"You tell Goose to send someone else next time, alright?"

"Aye, alright."

Richie sauntered out the room, down the hall and was met at the open front door by the bouncer. The bouncer looked over Richie's shoulder at Florida Al before he got out of Richie's way. When he did, Richie squinted against the light. Behind him, he could hear the grunting of blokes fucking turned right up.

He walked back the way he came, heading for the bus stop and pulling his trackie bottoms up every five minutes. Reckoned he'd have to do something about the gun. He didn't want to be walking somewhere, lose his pants *and* the weapon.

Richie leaned against the side of the bus stop, checked the times. Another hour or so, he'd be back at Goose's place, getting paid. Might be able to get down the dole for the afternoon at this rate. He pulled out his tabs, lit one. When he lifted his head, he saw a gang of charva lads coming his way. Three of them, wearing that same uniform of striped thin jumpers and trackie bottoms. One of them had a Berghaus over his jumper. Another one wore a cap, had box-whites on his feet and a hare lip. One of them, a lad with bad acne and worse teeth, saw Richie was smoking.

"How, mister," he said. "Got a tab?"

"Aye," said Richie. Reckoned these lads were getting the bus, he'd better give them as many tabs as they wanted, because he didn't want to hear the fucking whinge all the way back to Heworth. Richie held out the tabs. The vocal charva took one, tucked it behind his ear while the others moved around Richie.

"Got a light, like?"

Richie blew smoke, gave the lad his Bic. As he did, he felt something at his back. He turned, heard "Fuckin' hell" and saw the lad with the cap holding the dipped grip of the Magnum.

"How," said Richie. "That's —"

And Richie's vision exploded into white, pain flaring at the side of his head. He twisted, grabbed at the side of the bus shelter, his arse hitting the lean-seats and slipping. He dug his feet in, tried to keep upright. One hand up to his head, squinting through the explosions in his vision to see the smoking lad with a brick in his hand.

"The fuck you —"

The second blow knocked the struts out. Richie hit the ground as the kicking started. He cried out, brought his knees to his chest and tried to stay that way.

It was hard to dole out a proper meet-your-maker kicking when you were wearing trainers. And as Richie curled under the blow delivered by the smoking charva and his mates, he thanked a God he never really believed in for soft-toed shoes. The kicks still hurt, still battered fuck out of an already aching body, but they didn't tear him up like the boots he'd taken in the past. Whatever happened, however hard they went into him, he knew he'd live through this one, just as long as he stayed balled up and submissive.

Then, just as the rain of blows turned to a slow drizzle, Richie made the mistake of lifting his head a half-inch. A stray kick caught him in the temple, bounced his head off the road. He grunted as another foot knocked the air out of his lungs and he wrapped himself around the leg.

One more kick to the head snuffed his conscious mind.

Then it was flashes in the dark.

After that, just dark.

3

He could hear a baby crying somewhere.

As he struggled back to the world, he was positive he could hear a baby. He opened his eyes to slits, breathed out and felt his entire body seize up with pain.

The sound of the baby faded into silence.

It hadn't been a life-or-death beating, but that didn't mean he was going to run home. He had to take this slow. There was something in his hands. He looked down, saw a large white blob and tried to blink it into focus. He dropped the blob as he put one hand to the ground, spread his fingers and pushed. Lifted up to his knees, felt a strip of pain in his side as he tried to straighten up. Richie breathed out slowly. If his rib wasn't broken, it was bruised to fuck. So he leaned forward, stared at the blob on the ground, one arm supporting him, the other hanging loose by his side. He wanted to cry, but knew that would mean more pain.

So he set his jaw, breathed shallow through his nose. Thinking about those fucking charva cunts, and wondering where the fuck they'd come from. They went right for him like they had the scent, like they'd been *told*. And right enough, didn't Goose tell him that if Florida Al got the chance to fuck him over, he would?

Slowly, the white blob came into focus. A trainer, Nike. Would've been box-white if it wasn't for Richie's blood splattered across the instep. He picked up the shoe, held it to his chest as he tried to stand up. He dragged himself up onto one of the bus shelter seats and leaned there for a moment, staring at the chud stuck to the roof.

He was going to be alright. He just needed to work out what he was going to do next.

Richie reached into his pocket for his tabs. Found them gone. Along with everything else.

He expected the gun to go. He expected whatever money he had on him to go too. But they took his tabs, and that felt wrong somehow. Like Richie wasn't fucking human enough to need a tab after he had his arse handed to him. He still had the phone, though. Too old, not worth shit.

Goose told him to phone if there was any bother. Getting robbed struck Richie as bother, right enough, but he didn't dial. Instead, he tucked the phone into his trackie pocket and scanned the rest of the estate. Forgotten the last time he did a job for Goose. Richie was positive that wasn't going to happen again.

Phoning Goose wasn't going to change his situation. What was he going to say, that he got mugged? Goose would just tell him to go and get the gun back. Probably call him a stupid bastard into the bargain. The only thing that would change was that Goose would *know* Richie fucked up instead of suspecting it, and that would be future jobs out of the question. And even though he kept promising Becka that he'd go out there and get himself a proper job, he knew that the nine-to-five wasn't him, and even if he did manage to score some shift work in some grotty little shithole like a Macky-D's or something, he'd be getting a peanut wage for a shitty job. And there was still a part of Richie that held a deep, warm ambition for his life. That if he got in with decent company, he'd be set. And Goose was the only decent company he knew.

So it wasn't about this job, not really. It was about proving himself. Showing that he could be trusted to use his initiative when it all went to shit.

He pushed himself off the bus shelter seat, limped a few steps.

The entire estate looked deserted, but he knew someone must've seen him take his beating. And they did fuck all about it.

Typical of the Leam, he reckoned.

He kept walking, trying to minimise his limp. He didn't want to seem too hurt.

Especially not when he caught up with the little cunt whose shoe he was carrying.

4

"You forgot something, Cinders?"

Richie clamped a hand on the lad's arm and shoved the shoe into his startled face. The lad backed up quick, but only had so far to go before he hit the wall of the youth club.

This little prick wasn't hard to find — the lip wasn't something he could hide — but it still took hours. Richie had to take frequent breaks as he walked around the estate, ducking into boarded up doorways for a breather, a pause to exercise mind over matter, moving the pain to a dull ache with careful practice. It gave him time to think about how this was going to play out with the shoeless lad. How cool he was going to be, even what he'd say (that Cinders line was practised well in advance).

But not what he'd do when he saw the lad. Who he found propping up a youth club, smoking one of Richie's tabs and trying to look every inch a gangster. That dropped the moment Richie laid hands on him. And there was this rising tide of disgust when Richie got close up. The lad smelled of market aftershave, even though there was the barest hint of bumfluff on his cheeks. His skin was oily. And there was that stink you only got when you were scared out of your mind.

Richie rubbed the bottom of the trainer into the lad's face. The lad squirmed and tried to shout.

"Where is it?" said Richie.

"Dunno what you're talking about."

Richie dropped the shoe. Slapped the lad so hard it left a red mark that spread to the rest of the lad's face as he fought back the tears. "Don't fuckin' lie to us, son. You know exactly what I'm talking about. You and your mates, taken to beating the shit out of a bloke at a bus stop. Got more than you fuckin' bargained for, am I right?"

The lad shook his head over and over. "Wasn't me, man."

"Wasn't you?"

"Nah, you must've got us mixed up with someone else."

"Think I'm fuckin' daft, lad?"

"Nah."

"Think I'm a fuckin' spacka or something?"

"How —"

"You're the only charva hanging round here with a fuckin' *limp*. You get me?" Richie pointed at the lad's shoes. "So what happened to your foot?"

"Nowt," said the lad. "Got nowt to do with you, anyway."

Richie smacked the lad with his shoe. The lad took a moment to stare at the ground with tears in his eyes. His mouth was tight, lips invisible. Richie hoped to fuck that his mates weren't in the club, hoped that this mouthy little bastard wouldn't cry out for them. He glanced at the doorway of the youth club, then pulled the lad by his sweater round the back, hobbling the whole way. He never let go of that sweater. Knew the moment he did, this lad would rabbit, and Richie was in no state to give chase.

Richie slammed the lad against the back wall, held him at arm's length. "Well?"

"How, man, I fuckin' told you."

"How'd you get the limp?"

"Got a stone in me shoe."

"And how'd you get the blood on your track-ies?" said Richie, getting close up now. The lad opened his mouth, but Richie interrupted. "Where's the fuckin' gun?"

"Dunno —"

"Don't fuckin' lie to us. I'm telling you that right now. Take a second to think this through. You're talking to a gadgie you kicked shit out of and robbed. I'm not in the best of fuckin' moods, so this memory-loss shite isn't helping matters, you get me? I know you were there, and I know you robbed us because you're smoking my tabs. Now you also have to know, I wasn't carrying that gun around for protection, was I? If I wanted to use the thing, I would've popped the lot of you. Stands to reason I was carrying it for someone else then, doesn't it?"

The lad's face was blank.

"I'll tell you a name. Goose."

A twitch in the lad's face. Could've been a smile or a grimace, Richie didn't catch it in time.

"Aye, Goose. It's his gun. I haven't told him yet that he's had his gun nicked by a bunch of charva twats, but if I don't find out where it is, I might have to."

"Like fuck," said the lad.

Richie smiled, pulled out the mobile, and showed him the contact list of one. The lad closed his eyes as Richie replaced the mobile.

"Where is it?"

The lad's bottom lip threatened to swallow most of his face. Desperately trying not to cry. Obviously knew Goose by reputation, and Richie was impressed that the rep had travelled this far. But then the shitheads of the world tended to know their own. The lad screwed his face up suddenly, showed his bottom teeth and looked up the road. "Sold it."

"Sold it?"

The lad nodded.

"How the fuck did you *sell* it? It's been, what, a couple of fuckin' hours?"

"Had a gadgie lined up for one if we ever saw it."

So it wasn't Richie, he thought. It was anyone they saw coming out of Florida Al's place. It wasn't a conspiracy at all. The thought didn't comfort him as much as he hoped it would.

"Who?"

The lad shook his head, breathed out. Said, "There's this bouncer works The Admiral on the afternoons."

"Got a bouncer working the afternoons?"

The lad looked up. "You never been in The Admiral."

"What's his name?"

"Brandon."

"Is that first or last?"

"I dunno," said the lad. "It's all he told us, like."

"And this is the gadgie who's got the gun. You're sure about that?"

"Aye. How, I wouldn't lie to you, would I?"

"Course you fuckin' would. Because you've forgotten that I know where you hang out, and I can come back at any time. In fact, Goose can send people down here looking for you if he wants to. Even if you're not here, I'm sure one of your marras'll be quick to tell them where they can knock you up, what do you think?"

The lad frowned.

"Where's The Admiral?"

The lad gave him directions. It wasn't far.

"Good." Richie stepped back. The lad didn't move. "Now let's see what you've got in your pockets."

"I'm telling you, I *sold* the fuckin' gun."

"I don't doubt that, son. That's not why I'm telling you. Empty your fuckin' pockets. I want the cash you got for it, I want whatever else you got, and most of all I want my fuckin' tabs back."

The lad pulled a sour face, then started emptying his pockets. A nice wad of cash that wasn't anything to do with Richie, but which might've had something to do with the gun.

Then more cash on top of that.

"This your fuckin' job, is it?" said Richie. "The pay's mint."

The lad didn't say anything, kept turning out his pockets. Two lighters, one of them Richie's. His tabs. A mobile. Richie took the lot, then jerked his chin at the lad, said, "Now the shoe."

"Fuck you talking about?"

"Take your fuckin' shoe off. The foot you were kicking us with."

"I'm not taking nowt off."

Richie moved quick, pinned the lad to the wall. He drew back his fist, brought it hard and short into the lad's gut, then stepped back to watch him fold in half, the wind ripped out of him and the Gregg's steak bake he had for breakfast about to follow. Just as the lad went from the wet to dry heaves, Richie planted his foot in the lad's ribcage, feeling something crack against his instep. The lad let out a restrained howl, rolled over onto his side. Richie bent over, grabbed one of the lad's shoes and wrenched it off.

"When I tell you to take your fuckin' shoe off,

you take it off," said Richie, hefting the new shoe in his hand.

The lad burbled something on the ground. Richie waited until he was finished and looking his way, then he hurled the shoe as far as he could. It bounced off into a skip. Richie dusted his hands down, pulled out the lad's mobile and dropped it on the ground. Another shrill, fractured noise came out of the lad, getting higher as Richie brought his foot down on the mobile.

"Just in case you decide to call your mates round, eh?" said Richie.

He ground the pieces into the concrete, then turned out of the alley and headed for The Admiral. As he walked, he checked his watch. It was getting on for noon, which meant the place would be open at least.

Good, he thought. He could get a pint down his neck, and his hands were shaking enough to need one.

5

Early doors at The Admiral, and this Brandon gadgie still hadn't bothered his arse to turn up. Didn't matter. Richie could wait for him inside. He'd just have to hope that the charva lad didn't find some way to warn the bouncer that Richie was coming. Course, Richie wasn't daft — he wasn't about to pick a fight with a bloke who fought on a nightly basis. Not in his condition. Nah, he thought he'd see how well a little gentle persuasion went first.

Richie pushed through stiff and thin double doors into The Admiral, which didn't look so much like a pub as someone's front room with pretensions. It was already heavily populated, clusters of smoking men ignoring the ban, huddled over thick pints of bitter and flat lager. The entire place stank of dog. Richie went straight for the bar. A stringy pale man with a shaved head stared at him.

"Pint of Carling," said Richie.

The skinny man didn't move. "How old are you?"

"You what?"

"You heard."

"I'm eighteen, mate."

"Just turned, is it?"

"Nah." Richie looked at the bloke with dead eyes as he bluffed it. "Closer to nineteen, you want to know, like."

"That right?" said the landlord. He breathed in and smiled it out. "This is a member's club, son."

"It's a pub. Now give us a pint of Carling before I put your fuckin' teeth out."

The landlord bared his teeth as if he'd tasted something rotten. It looked like an invitation to Richie. Then he looked behind Richie and blinked.

"Your man's not in yet." Richie smiled.

The landlord brought his focus to the lad at his bar. "The fuck happened to your face?"

"The fuck happened to yours?"

The landlord's eyes narrowed to a double squint. Richie raised one hand and grinned as wide as he could with the swelling.

"I'm just having you on, mate," he said. "I'm here to talk to Brandon."

"Brandon."

"Aye. Me and him, we got a little business."

"Kind of business?"

"Nowt bad. Nowt illegal. And we'll take it outside."

"Good," said the landlord. "I don't want your blood on me nice new carpet."

Richie glanced down. The carpet wasn't nice or new. In fact, he was positive that was where the dog smell was coming from.

"He's not here," said the landlord.

"I know he's not here. I said that. I want a pint while I'm waiting, mind. If it's not too much trouble."

The landlord thought about saying something — Richie could see it flicker in his face —

but then shook it out of his head. He went to the pumps, set a Carling to pour. Richie dug in his pocket, brought out a twenty and slapped it on the bar. "What whisky you got? I can't see from here."

"Bell's or Grouse."

"Any brandy?"

"Nah."

"Then give us a Grouse, double, no ice." He nodded at the note. "You keep the change an' all."

When the landlord slid the Grouse and pint in front of Richie, he looked around the place for somewhere to sit. Took him a while to find somewhere with a decent view of the entrance and the car park, and he knew it could change in a minute flat. People were as territorial as wolves in this place and might've marked that territory in the same way judging from the smell of the nook Richie found. He just hoped that some old bugger wouldn't get mouthy if he saw Richie in his seat.

Halfway down the pint, Richie noticed that his hands had finally stopped trembling. He set them both flat on the table in front of him, looked like he was about to conduct a one-man séance, then balled them up into fists. Looked again — still no shakes. He looked out of the window. That was lucky. He'd kept his hands hidden most of the time he'd talked to the landlord, but he wouldn't be able to hide the shakes from Brandon.

That was if the bugger ever turned up. Richie started to gnaw on the inside of his mouth, glancing across at the landlord. Because if that bloke over there was clock-watching, then it meant that Brandon wasn't the type of bloke to stumble in late. Which meant there could be something wrong already.

He knew he shouldn't be thinking like this already, but it was habit. The old saying — pessimists are rarely disappointed. In Richie's case, he reckoned if he saw the worst in the situation, it minimised the surprise when life chucked shit at him. He looked into his pint, reckoned that he'd give Brandon until the end of the beer to turn up, then he'd try to get the bloke's address off the landlord. In the meantime, he had to sit tight, play it calm and collected.

It was difficult. If he sat alone in silence, he had a tendency to think. And when he thought, he reckoned he should be at the dole office right now, keeping that promise to Becka. She wasn't even the type to guilt him into going, but she'd gotten fucking responsible while he was inside, hinting at the kind of life she wanted to have. At first, Richie reckoned she'd seen one too many Jeremy Kyles and had the straight scared into her, but Becka kept on. She didn't nag. Didn't need to. She told him what she wanted like it was an achievable dream. Respectability, not in the house-in-the-suburbs kind of way, not really. More in the boyfriend's-not-in-the-nick vein.

"I want you around," she said.

"I am around," he told her.

"Aye, until you do something stupid and get caught."

He tried it on with the charm, said, "I'll just not get caught next time."

"Nah," she said. "I don't want that."

"Becka —"

"I can't take that, Richie. I need promises, and I need 'em kept, alright?"

"I can promise."

"*And* kept, I said." She did one of her big sighs at that, like that tart in the big frilly dress from that pure long film they watched the Sunday before he went in. Everything was so fucking *tiring*. "I need someone who's going to be around, someone who's not going to jail, like, at a second's notice."

And Richie said, "Alright."

"You promise?" she said.

"Yeah, aye."

"'Cause I'll hold you to it."

He noticed the tears about to come, so he said, "Aye, I promise."

They went into a hug. Richie felt her shaking against his chest. For a second, he wondered if she was laughing, and then wondered what the fuck he'd just agreed to. He moved away and saw the tears running down her face. He frowned, asked her what the matter was. She shook her head, smiling, then went back to his chest.

His chest ached now, the memory turned her hug into a headbutt. Richie rubbed his cheek and stared out of the window, seeing nothing. The way she looked at him after he promised, the way she started talking about moving somewhere else, somewhere Richie could get himself a proper job, all this talk of settling down. It made his gut twitch.

And Richie said, "How, hang on a sec, we can't move anywhere, can we? I'm still on licence."

"We can work round that," she said. "Reckon the probation'll be happy you're moving away from the reason you got put inside. Besides, we'll need to be in a decent area, lots of parks an' that. Like, a family area."

It was all falling into place now. And he wondered how the fuck he'd managed to miss it. Too caught up in trying to find paying work, most likely, but when he thought about it now, she wasn't being too fucking coy about it, was she? The lass was either pregnant or wanting to get there. And Richie'd promised no more dodgy jobs, as good as he promised to fucking marry her.

"Fuck," he said now. An old guy at the next table turned his paper bag face Richie's way, his mouth working. "Nah, man. Not you."

Richie leaned forward on the table, put his head in his hands and stared straight down into his barely fizzing pint. If he'd known sooner, he wouldn't have gone to Goose. He would've got himself down the dole and signed on. Would've took the first job they gave him and worked it till he broke.

And now where was he? Some shitty pub miles away from home, waiting on a bloke who had a gun he needed. A fucking *gun*. Richie never saw a real live gun before in his life until today. Knew some of the lads further up the food chain wore the vests and carried something in their cars, but Richie'd never come into full contact with them. Now in the course of a single morning, he'd bought and lost one.

This was the way he kept promises, was it?

He caught movement, looked up and saw a brown Cavalier rolling into the car park. A big bloke behind the wheel, almost took up the front two seats by himself. He killed the engine, then struggled to get out of the car. Then Richie noticed that he wasn't just a big bloke, but a big *fat* bloke. Muscle underneath all that, mind. Not like Florida Al. If anyone looked like a bouncer, it was this bloke.

Richie watched Brandon stride towards the front of the pub, then downed his Grouse. It burned going down and Richie wanted to cough it out, but he held firm. Brandon pushed into the pub, and the landlord called him over. Richie heard the landlord say something about "the lad in the corner", and Brandon say, "Oh aye?"

Richie hunkered up around his pint, breathing slow, pushing thoughts of Becka and the possible bairn out of his head.

"You wanted to talk to us, son?" said Brandon.

Richie turned in his seat, looked up at the bouncer. From this angle, the gadgie was a fucking mountain.

"Aye," he said. "Probably best we do it outside, like."

And he finished his pint, got out of his seat, and tried not to limp as he led the way.

6

Brandon thought about it for a long time, looking up at the grey sky, his lips bunched. Then he looked down at Richie.

"Nah," he said.

Richie opened his arms, tried to smile. "Howeh, I'm just trying to offer you a fuckin' deal here, mate."

"How's it I'm your fuckin' mate?" Brandon's mouth hung open. "I don't know you, but you're all acting pally like you fuckin' know us, like. I never seen you before in my life. And now you're talking about a dangerous fuckin' weapon. A gun, was it?"

"Air pistol."

"Right, *air* pistol."

"Converted."

"That's it. Now why would I buy something like that?" Brandon rolled his shoulders back. "Like I need a fuckin' gun, I got enough going for *me*."

Richie nodded. "Aye, I know. But I also know you bought a gun from a charva lad this morning."

"Nah."

"He told us you did."

"Oh aye? What's his name then?"

Richie blinked at Brandon, felt his face burn up. Course he didn't know the lad's name. Should've found that out, shouldn't he? Fuck's sake. Took one beating and his head was all over the fucking place. Richie grinned the embarrassment out of his system, waiting to lose the blush as he stared at the tarmac. "Don't matter what his name was, Brandon, does it?"

"Aye, it does. You don't know his fuckin' name, you're making all this up."

"I know *your* name."

"So?"

"Where d'you reckon I got it from?"

"The fuck am I supposed to know?"

"From the lad who sold you the gun. The Magnum."

"Oh, it's a fuckin' *Magnum* now, is it?" Brandon's face only half broke into something that could pass for amusement. This bloke couldn't lie for shit. "See, now you got all confused. Because before it was just a converted air pistol, now it's a fuckin' Magnum? Seriously, I don't know what you're talking about, mate. But I do know, you keep talking to us with that fuckin' tone, we're going to have issues."

"Why's that?"

"I don't need a gun."

"But you got one."

"There y'are again with the tone."

"How, fuckin' *look* at yourself, man. You're lying through your teeth. I know you bought a gun this morning, I was going to offer to buy it back off you, but the way I'm thinking now, fuck it, I'll let Goose pick it up himself."

"Goose? Haddaway and shite, man."

"Nah, I'm telling you. I'm working for —"

"For a goose," said Brandon. "Right. You're out your fuckin' box, marra."

Richie stared at the bouncer. Aye, this bloke didn't have the first fucking clue who he was dealing with. And part of Richie wanted to let it lie, sic Goose or whoever Goose sent — probably the heavyweights everyone called the Gallaghers — get down here and bray fuck out of Brandon The Bouncer. He was a proper doorknob, this one, with his number two on his head, puffer jacket, signets on one hand, wedding ring on the other.

"You married?" said Richie.

"Fuck kind of question's that?"

He jerked his head. "Noticed the ring."

Brandon bristled slightly. Looked like he was expecting a fight, waiting for the inevitable your-missus-is-a-fucking-hooer slight. When there didn't appear to be one coming, Brandon glanced down at the ring and said, "Aye, I'm married, like."

"Any kids?"

"Fuck off."

"I'm just asking."

"Why?"

"Because," said Richie. "This bloke I'm working for, the bloke whose gun you have, he'll send some lads down here to get it back —"

"Oh aye, right."

"Aye. I'm not one of them lads, either. I'm just a courier. All I did was buy the gun and I'm bringing it to him. I'm not a fighter. Only need to look at us to know that. But my point is, them lads that Goose sends down, they won't just stop with you. Your wife'll get her face mashed up, maybe get a wrist broke into the bargain. I don't know what else. Depends on who's sent. And if you've got kids —"

Brandon put a hand on Richie then, shoved him in the shoulder. There was power behind the move. Richie nearly went on his arse. He held up both hands.

"Wait a second —"

"You threatening us, you little cunt?"

"No, you *listen* to us, you'll know I'm not. Look at us. You think I'm the kind of lad who'd threaten someone like you? I'm not going to risk it, am I? Only thing that I'm interested in is getting the gun back. I've got money, you can have your money back, full fuckin' refund. But I need that gun."

Brandon ran his tongue under his bottom lip, breathing through his nose. Richie could tell this wasn't what he'd planned for the afternoon. What Brandon wanted was an excuse to kick off. He couldn't rightly batter the shit out of Richie without Richie kicking off first, though. Some kind of bouncer's code, the way Brandon was used to dealing with people. All this logic shite was doing his brain in. Thing was, even as a chill breeze picked up and numbed the aching bruises on his face, Richie was optimistic. Even willing to offer the cash he had on him. Anything to get out of this as peacefully as possible.

Then Brandon shook his head. "Nah, I don't think so."

"What?"

"I heard what you said. Appreciate your concern. But I reckon, whoever the fuck this Goose gadgie is, he can come down here and do whatever. I got mates who'll step up if it comes to it."

Richie half-smiled, couldn't believe it. Wanted to give this bloke examples he'd listen to. If Goose's lads came down to the Leam, it wouldn't be a fucking *West Side Story* face-off, it would be this Brandon bloke squealing through the blood in his mouth in the middle of the night. "I don't think you get it."

"I get it," said Brandon. "You're working for some half-arse hard man from where, like, north of the fuckin' river, right?"

"He's not half-arsed," said Richie.

"Aye, well, whatever the fuck you want to tell us, I think I'm going to keep hold of what I bought."

Richie's smile went full beam as he reached for his tabs. He stuck one in his mouth and lit it. "I thought you didn't have it."

"Nah, mate, *you're* the one doesn't have it. And you're not getting it, neither, so do yourself a fuckin' favour and fuck off, alright? Get back to fuckin' school. Some of us have got real work to do."

Richie blew smoke. "Fuck's that supposed to mean?"

"Means I've got a real job. Not skivvying for some cunt." Brandon slapped the chest of his puffer jacket. "I'm legit, mate."

"Aye," said Richie, nodding.

"Now fuck off."

Brandon didn't put hands on him again, but he made out as if he was going to, which flinched Richie back a step. Then Brandon turned back to The Admiral, his hands tucked deep into his puffer. Richie took the tab from his mouth, watching the bouncer return to his post. Brandon stopped at the double doors, pushed one of them open and shouted something inside. Then he assumed the usual position outside the pub.

Richie kept watching him. He smoked the rest of his tab, then started walking towards the pub. His eyes never left Brandon, who started to look more irritated the closer Richie got. Wondering what the fuck this lad had to say to him, probably thinking that he'd already said it all and getting angry that he'd have to repeat himself. When Richie got to the double doors, Brandon stuck out a hand. "I don't think so."

"Why not?"

"Landlord doesn't want you in there. You're under age."

"It was you I wanted to talk to."

"And we talked. You got nowt to say to us."

"Give us the gun."

Brandon laughed and spit fell over his lip. He wiped it away and said, "Go on, mate. Off you go."

"I'm not asking anymore. I'm not even offering you your money back. I'm telling you. Give us the gun back."

Brandon leaned forward, got right in Richie's face. He could smell the mixture of chewing gum and gin on the bouncer's breath as he said, "Fuck. Off."

Richie swung. Clocked the bouncer on the side of the head, right in the ear, threw him off balance, but didn't do much damage. Didn't matter. Richie lunged for Brandon, planted both hands on the man's torso, and shoved him hard against the double doors. Brandon didn't get a chance to right himself, and his weight carried him through the doors. As he hit the carpet, the doors clattered shut.

The noise was like a starter's pistol. Richie turned to the car park, started running.

He hadn't felt anything under that jacket. Nothing that could've been a gun, anyway.

Which meant the gun was probably still in the bastard's shit-brown Cavalier.

As he approached the car, he looked around for a half-brick, something to put through the window. Nothing in sight — The Admiral's landlord kept the carpark spotless. Probably sick of having his windows put out by drunks. Richie glanced that way now, saw movement inside the pub.

Brandon gearing up to beat the shit out of him.

No time. Richie pulled the sleeve of his hoodie over his right hand and weighed up the driver's side window.

7

As soon as Richie put his hand through the window, he remembered that he should have used his elbow. Pain jolted from his knuckles up his forearm. When he tried to pull the hand free, something dug in and held him in place. He felt something tear, saw blood blossom on the hoodie's sleeve and fought to stay conscious. He'd already dropped out once today. He didn't fancy hitting the deck again, especially considering the commotion in The Admiral.

Richie panicked, wrenched his hand through the shattered window, the end of his sleeve sopping with blood, the sound of glass pebbles skittering across the ground, and a thick nausea rising slowly in his gut. He reached in with his left, unlocked the driver's door and bent over to get a better look. He flipped open the glove compartment, swept out the crap Brandon kept in there — gum, maps, petrol receipts, old and unmarked cassettes. It spilled onto the passenger seat, dropped onto the floor of the car.

No gun.

Richie turned, looked behind him. He heard shouting, but couldn't focus. Looked like there were people coming out of The Admiral. He could make out the big black puffer jacket, assumed the rest were those mates Brandon was talking about.

Back to the car. Richie looked in the back seat of the Cavalier, sticking his left hand down between the seats and immediately wishing he hadn't when his fingers came back sticky.

It had to be in here somewhere. Unless Brandon bought the gun, dropped it off at home before he came to work on his shift. And if that was the case, then why would he need the gun? A bloke could protect himself a lot easier at home than he could on the doors. Richie had reckoned the reason this bloke bought the gun was as an added equalizer on the job. Christ knew what the kids were like round here, and Richie knew the adults were probably a lot worse. But if he'd stashed the gun somewhere else, then that was Richie fucked. There'd be no way of getting it back then. He'd have to go back to Goose empty-handed, and he didn't want to think about that.

He checked under the back seats. Nothing. Swore under his breath.

Behind him, Brandon was halfway across the car park and about to break into a run. Richie felt under the driver's seat, found nothing but a scrap of what looked like an old porn mag. Then he caught a glimpse of a black shape under the passenger seat. He stretched out his left to grab at it when pain exploded at the back of his head. Richie jerked forward, felt the bottom of the car doorframe jab into his chest. The breath shot out of him.

"Fuckin' thieving *cunt*."

Richie twisted to see Brandon put his boot into Richie's gut. The nausea that'd previously sat there now burst up his throat. Richie grabbed onto the metal frame under the passenger seat and spewed onto the driver's side. A moment's recoil from Brandon before he brought his foot down on Richie's bloody hand.

The pain yanked Richie to full consciousness. He screamed, whipped his hand out from under Brandon's foot and dug in, dragged himself across the bottom of the car.

There it was. Under the passenger seat.

Richie grabbed the grip of the Magnum, clattered it against the seat frame and screamed as he brought it out, pointed at Brandon.

Brandon didn't get a chance to recognise the gun before Richie pulled the trigger.

There was a loud, dry crack, and Brandon's head snapped backwards in a pink mist. His legs went out from under him and the bouncer hit the ground in a heap.

Then everything was silent apart from the ringing in Richie's ears, the thud of his heart beating double-time and his breath, rasping hard and painful.

Richie shrugged out of the car, hit the ground

in a sitting position. His right hand lay pulped on the tarmac. He couldn't move it. The blood had stained the sleeve of his hoodie brown as it dried. Richie looked up at the gang of Brandon's mates. Or acquaintances, seeing as Richie recognised them all from the pub. The landlord with the shaved head seemed to have lost ten years, looking at Richie like a scared kid. Richie brought the gun up, aimed at the landlord.

"Hang on a sec, mate, it's alright. It's okay. We're all fine here, right?"

Richie felt like crying, but he kept breathing hard so he wouldn't. He drew a bead on the landlord and for a second his finger tightened around the trigger. Not enough to fire.

"Fuck off," he said to the blokes gathered round. "Go on."

Richie kicked at the tarmac, pushed himself up to his feet, his right arm hanging by his side. He kept the gun trained on the men as they backed off to the pub. There was blood in his mouth. He tried to summon up some gob and spat the mixture at the ground.

Brandon wasn't going anywhere. Laid out on

his back, one of his legs tucked under him, the other straight out. A mess where his right eye socket used to be. Blood streaked out behind him on the ground. When Richie saw that, his left hand started shaking again and he started breathing through his teeth. It was impossible to breathe through his nose. The smell out here was too bad.

Richie wiped his mouth with the back of his gun hand. Wouldn't be long now, someone would've called the polis, and the fucking Armed Response would be on its way. As if a five-year mandatory for carrying this bastard gun wasn't bad enough, he now had a fucking murder charge to think about.

And he was thinking about it too much. The ache from his hand clouded his brain, the shock of what had just happened doubly so. He closed his eyes for a moment, thought he was going to drop out, then caught himself.

He had to move. He had to get out of here. A fucking dead body and a smoking gun. Somewhere out there on the estate, he thought he could hear sirens.

8

He didn't want to chuck an eppy in the middle of the Macky-D's, but if that fat bastard in front of him didn't get his arse shifted quick-smart, Richie was going to use what little strength he had left to put a boot up his ring. He'd been alternating his stare between the two-inch roll of back flab that poked out from under the fat lad's toon strip and the angry, pulsing zit on the back of his neck. Meanwhile, Porky fucking Pig was hemming and hawing about whether to have a second meal, and Richie wasn't getting any healthier.

"How," said Richie.

Fat Lad didn't react.

"You," said Richie.

Still nothing.

"How, ya fat cunt. I'm talking to you."

Fat Lad started to turn around. It took a while because he was playing it like a hard man.

"You want to move this along?" said Richie. "Some of us got places to be."

Fat Lad looked like he was about to say something. Then he got a proper eyeful of Richie and he worked his mouth. Reckoned maybe that the one super-size was enough for now. Fat Lad dropped his gaze to the floor, then nodded, grabbed his tray and shuffled off. Didn't say anything. Didn't need to — his face said it all. And when Richie moved up to the counter, he reckoned that face must be fucking catching, because the Macky-D's employee had the same expression, like someone just dumped a load in his kecks.

"Ehm, give us a *large* strawberry milkshake there, please mate. And some chips an' all."

The lad behind the counter didn't move. Staring at Richie, and he knew there was plenty to stare at. He was pretty sure he had blood on his face, and he knew for a stone-cold that there was a big red wet patch coming through the bottom of his hoodie. Richie reckoned he probably looked like he was gut-shot. His right sleeve hung useless, and there was the bump of his crooked arm under the hoodie. On top of that, he heard the *spat-spat-spat* of his blood hitting the floor. This lad in front of him probably wondered who was going to clean it up, and whether it was a health and safety issue. Because this scared lad didn't know that Richie wasn't positive, did he? The way Richie must've looked right now — pale, drawn, skinny as grass — there was every possibility that the lad behind the counter already figured him for a smackhead. And career smackheads aren't known for their impeccable health.

"You deaf, mate?"

"Huh?" said the lad.

"Says I want a milkshake and chips."

"Right," said the lad. "Eat in or —"

"Take out. Give us a shitload of napkins an' all, will you?"

The lad looked like he was about to heave a sigh of relief. Richie reckoned he even caught a smile on the lad's face as he told Richie how much it was. He already knew; he had the right money ready, paying with his left hand. He watched the lad grab one of the paper sacks and set Richie's milkshake going as he went for the chips.

That sack was what Richie really wanted. Everything else was a bonus, a way of keeping his energy levels up, because it felt like he was bleeding hard. But there was a gun weighing the back of his trackies down and he really wanted to hold that thing at arm's length.

So he was uncomfortable, made worse by feeling like he's the centre of attention in here. Used to be, this was a normal Macky-D's, but now they've gutted the place, thrown lime green on a couple of walls, giant photo-murals of pebbles or some shit on the others. All the tables and chairs that were previously bolted to the floor were gone now, replaced with brown pleather half-booths. Richie reckoned it looked more fair trade than fast food. Trying to fool the wankers, most likely.

And the wankers were out in force today.

Most of them ghouls, giving Richie sidelongs because of the spreading stain. Part of him wanted to kick off, force them into minding their own fucking business, but he knew kicking off wouldn't help matters. First sign of care in the community, there'd be fingers tapping nine on mobiles all through the place. And Christ, if Richie cracked up now, the fucking polis'd be on him like the Fat Lad on his Big Mac. Maybe even quicker than that — Richie thought he remembered seeing a couple of uniforms walking up Northumberland Street a few minutes ago. But he couldn't be sure of much, not with the blood loss fucking with his head.

He needed to maintain. And even if this lad behind the counter was taking his sweet time coming up with a simple order, there was no sense in losing his rag.

"There y'are," said the lad.

Richie looked up, saw the bag. He tried a smile on for size. From the look on the lad's face, the smile had the desired effect.

Aye, everyone was happy now that Richie was on his way out the door, even if he was leaving a staggered blood trail behind him.

Soon as he was outside, he strode across Northumberland Street, swerving through the cross-stream of people who barely look at him, and heading for the long, sloped alley that runs up the side of Marks and Sparks. The alley led to an entrance to Eldon Square that nobody used, but it was lined with alcoved shutters. When Richie reckoned he was safe, he leaned against the wall, turned in towards it. He breathed out, and his head started to spin. Too much exertion crossing the road, got his heart pumping too fast.

He had to remember — his heart pumped too fast, he'd bleed out quicker; too slow, and he'd pass out. Had to maintain a balance if he was going to make it out of this.

He kept breathing. Slow and sure. Waiting for the dizziness to pass. His eyes closed.

Then he pulled open the paper bag, removed the milkshake, set it down on the ground. The chips, he wedged between his hip and the alcove wall. He leaned forward a little, checked to see if anyone was about to come his way. Then he removed the gun from the back of his trackies and held it by the trigger guard. The smell was a giveaway that it'd recently been fired, but only if you gave it a good sniff. Plus, Richie was hoping that the smell of chips would mask it a bit. He put the gun against his thigh, pulled out the large wad of napkins, and started to wipe the metal down. When half the napkins had been used, and when Richie was happy that the gun was as clean as it was going to be, he eased the weapon into the bag. Then he took the rest of the napkins and stuck them under his hoodie. There was a sudden jab of pain as he broke the blood seal on his hand. He held the napkins tight to the wound, waited it out.

Richie stared at the bag as he waited for the pain to go. Then he removed his hand, grabbed a handful of chips and stuffed them into his mouth. His gut reacted badly, threatening to throw them straight back up. He stopped, froze, willing himself to keep the food down. Then he picked up the shake, thumbed off the lid and took a hefty gulp. After a few minutes of concentrated eating and drinking, his stomach got

9

Richie sat on the Metro, one of the double seats on the side, a copy of the free newspaper in his lap to cover up most of the blood, as well as the bag with the gun in it. He stared through the gap in the bodies at his reflection in the opposite window. Saw the concrete give way to night, the train pulling out from Byker and heading out towards the coast.

He shifted his gaze, squinted at the Metro map above the doors. Counted the stops until he had to get off.

Six.

Chilly Road. Walkergate. Wallsend. Hadrian Road. Howdon. Percy Main.

Then he had to get off the train. Which meant

he'd have to start thinking about movement when he got to Howdon. He'd have to psyche himself up, really concentrate, because since he managed to barge his way into this seat at Monument, the last thing he wanted to do was leave it. The train was packed, too, full of people who wanted to nip in there if he so much as flinched. If he could've moved to check his watch, it would have been about five o'clock, he reckoned. It was dark and cold outside, and he couldn't look anywhere on this train without seeing a suit or skirt. The fuckers had tried to guilt him into moving seats instead of taking up two on his own, but their first glimpse of blood was enough to cut that short. Now they were just avoiding eye contact and willing him to move.

Not that Richie really noticed. He was too busy thinking. Wondering if he'd make it to The Well without bleeding out on the Metro. Wondering if he'd be caught before that happened, some civic-minded cunt with a mobile calling him out because he didn't fit the bill of something they wanted to look at on their way home from work.

No, that couldn't happen. And he was pretty sure he'd be alright between town and Goose's house. If he spent hours wandering the Leam looking for a bus stop and nothing happened to him then, it shouldn't happen now he was close to home turf. Now he just had to figure out what he was going to do when he got to Goose's.

Everything Becka told him, it was one hundred percent on the fucking nail. And he only now started to get it into his head that there wasn't a future with Goose. The man didn't remember Richie's previous job, didn't even twitch when Richie mentioned it, so it didn't matter what he did, because Richie wasn't going to be anything but a fucking skivvy. Just like Becka said. And just like he'd always be unless he did something about it.

And he definitely did something about it. He looked down, saw a picture of a blonde Amy Winehouse on the front of the free newspaper. She looked all bedraggled and distraught, hustled to court to see her bloke, and Richie thought, *you think you've got problems, love*.

He had the gun. That should be enough for

Goose. The bloke didn't have a rep for caring about his employees, but he should be happy enough with his gun. And as Richie thought about it now, he reckoned that there was no reason he shouldn't be able to just walk out of the place. It wasn't like Richie was going to get another job, especially after the time it took to sort this one out. And then he got to thinking that this stupid fucking errand was a blessing in disguise. He wouldn't have thought about jacking it in if it hadn't been for this nightmare of a day, and now he was. It was probably a sign that he should've been doing something better with his life, just like Becka wanted him to.

The train slowed and Richie looked out the window. Wallsend. Three to go.

A thick crowd of commuters got off the Metro. Richie nodded to himself, catching a full reflection of himself in the window. He was pale, and while he hoped it was just the light in the carriage, he knew it wasn't. A brief look down at his hoodie under the paper confirmed it. He was still bleeding, so much he'd stained the seat between his legs.

His hand was a mess, his fingers already broken by the car window, the skin torn on chunks of glass. But when Brandon started grinding Richie's bones, that was the last of it. Now it didn't even feel like Richie had a right hand — just a huge mass of pain on the end of his right arm now. He knew he shouldn't be going to Goose's place right now, not if he wanted to get out of this without any lasting damage. He knew he should've got his arse down to the hospital. But then he figured he'd made it this far, so what the fuck.

Now he started to have second thoughts. He could feel the energy leeching out of him as he sat there. Feeling his brain get locked in one thought. He looked up the carriage, saw a baby in a pushchair. The baby had a tuft of ginger hair in a tiny bunch on the top of its head, and was staring intently at Richie.

Richie blinked. The baby jerked in the pushchair. Then he looked at the rubber floor of the train.

When he looked up again, he turned back to the baby, but it was gone. Now he didn't know where the train was. He didn't catch the last stop. Part of him panicked, thought he'd missed his stop. He twisted around in his seat to look out of the window, see if he could catch any landmarks. The free paper slipped from his lap to the floor, and the ache in his side flared into searing pain. Richie doubled up, sucking breath through his teeth.

If he missed his stop, he wasn't sure he'd be able to get back to The Well. Because that would mean changing, hanging round the Metro stop until the next train, and Richie wasn't sure he had that kind of time left.

He felt the train start to slow, and bobbed his head at the window, trying to see beyond the reflection of the lights in here. He shifted in his seat, his cheek almost to the window, trying to see up ahead.

It was his stop. He breathed out quickly and a dart of pain shot through his ribs.

When Richie turned back, the woman sitting opposite was staring at Richie's hoodie with her mouth a perfect little O. He looked down, noticed that the bloodstain had spread up to the middle of his chest.

"Are you alright?" she said.

Richie tried to laugh, but it came out wrong, sounded like a cat with a hairball. He still managed a smile, shaking his head slowly from side to side as he grabbed onto the handrail. The Macky-D's bag was pinched between thumb and forefinger. It swayed too much for Richie's nerves, so he leaned his shoulder against the rail, got a better grip on the bag.

"Aye," he said. "I'm just fuckin' dandy, like."

The train lurched to a stop. There was the hiss of doors, then the clatter as they opened. Richie pushed himself from the rail and walked out onto the platform. A voice behind him told him to stand clear of the doors, please. Then the train glided out of the station.

Richie watched the Metro leave. Then he turned to look at the estate.

It wasn't a long walk to Goose's house, but Richie knew it'd feel like miles.

He fumbled for a tab, the last one in the pack, lit it, then headed for the concrete steps that took him down to the road.

10

Richie was surprised to notice that Goose's house hadn't changed in the slightest since this morning. It felt like so much had happened to him, it should've happened elsewhere, too. But then life wasn't that fucking fair, was it?

He leaned on the doorbell, and the big bastard they called Noel because of the unibrow answered the door. This bloke was one of Goose's lads, one of the Gallaghers, did Goose's dirty work and did it with fucking relish. But Richie wasn't intimidated. He grinned.

"Y'alright?" said Noel. Then, seeing all the blood as he got closer. "Jesus fuckin' Christ, man, you can't come round here looking like that."

"It's nowt," said Richie. "It's dried. Just an accident, anyway. Goose told us to pick something up for him, like. I got it here."

He held up the Macky-D's bag. Noel frowned.

"He told you to get him a Macky-D's?"

"It's from Al. On the Leam."

Noel looked out at the street, then held the door open for Richie. "Get inside. If you fuckin' pass out, we're dumping you somewhere, you know that. Can't be having ambulances round here. Bring the fuckin' polis with 'em now, don't they?"

Richie stumbled into the house, using the wall as a guide as he headed for the front room. There was the smell of cooking in the air, like someone had been boiling vegetables. When Richie got to the front room, he saw Goose sitting with a Sunday dinner on the tray in front of him — roast beef, gravy, roasties, peas, carrots and what looked like cabbage. He wondered what fucking day it was now. Thought it was a weekday, but Goose's meal just threw him right off. Goose had a fork halfway to his mouth when he saw Richie and stopped.

"The fuck are you doing in here like that?" he said, putting the fork down.

Richie held out the Macky-D's bag. "Got your gun. Went and saw Florida Al."

"He do that to you?"

Richie shook his head. "Nah, that's a different story."

"You want to tell it?"

"You want the fuckin' gun or not?"

Goose nodded to Noel, who took the bag off Richie. Noel held the bag at the bottom and peered inside.

"Aye, there's your gun," said Noel. He pulled out the weapon with one hand, crumpling the bag up with the other. He handed the gun to Goose, grip first.

"He give you any shit?" said Goose.

Richie leaned against the door jamb. He thought about the question, and then shook his head again. "Al didn't do nowt but make us look at gay porn."

Noel laughed. It was a sound that came from his gut.

"Aye," said Goose, "he'll do that, right enough.

And you paid him and everything went alright?"

"Yeah, aye, everything went tickety-boo at Al's place."

Goose twirled a finger at Richie. "So what happened then?"

"Little accident," said Richie.

"Little?"

"Nowt special."

"Looks like you're going to keel over," said Goose.

"How much did we say?"

"For what?"

"For delivery." Richie found it hard to focus now. The dim light in the room was a contrast from the train, and it was doing his head in. Things in his direct vision were crystal clear, then blurry as fuck. It was like a bad drunk all the time. He licked his dry lips. "For the gun."

"What about the bullets?" said Goose.

Richie didn't say anything.

"He try to short you on them?"

Richie looked at the bloke in the wheelchair through narrowed eyes. It was about the only way he could keep looking at him. He wondered if Goose had been tipped already. If this was some kind of trap.

Finally, Richie breathed out, attempted a shrug. "I don't know. I didn't check."

"What'd I tell you?"

"I know what you told us."

"I said check for fuckin' bullets, didn't I?"

"And you never told us how I was supposed to do that."

Goose worked his mouth. He cracked open the revolver. Frowned. "That fuckin' bastard."

"What is it?" said Noel.

"He's taking the piss, that fat old poof. Seen what he's done here? He's only loaded the gun but one, hasn't he? Fuckin' bastard'll short you *one* bullet, save a pound and tell you who's boss. Tell, that flabby arse bandit's going to get his one day, I swear to fuckin' God."

"How much did we say?" said Richie again, this time louder.

"Noel, give him a fifty or something, will you?"

Noel's face was pinched as he went into the back pocket of his jeans, pulled out an orange and handed it to Richie. Richie looked at the note, wrinkled and smudged with something that he didn't want to think about. He nodded slowly to himself. This was what it was all about, eh? Fifty fucking quid to replace a right hand.

"Got more work for you if you want it," said Goose, but Richie was already shaking his head.

"Don't want it," he said.

"Don't want it? Fuckin' hell, this morning you was *demanding* a job."

Richie pushed himself off the doorjamb, held out his left hand to steady himself.

"Now look at him," said Goose, tucking the Magnum down the side of his chair. "He spends one day on the Leam and he's a fuckin' wreck. Here, son, you get yourself seen to and I'll give you a bell later on in the week, see if I can't hook you up with something lucrative, eh?"

Richie moved into the hall, still shaking his head. "Don't bother."

"Here, hang on a sec, I didn't tell you that you could go. So don't you fuckin' dare think you can leave just yet."

Richie stopped in the dark hallway. He stared at the pattern on the carpet.

"It was Al that shorted us, wasn't it?" said Goose.

"Aye," said Richie.

"Wouldn't be that you got yourself a fuckin' gun and lost your mind out there, would it?"

"Dunno what you mean."

"You do. There's one bullet missing."

"I know that. Now."

"Just need to make sure you're not playing funny buggers with us."

"And I told you," said Richie, without a word of a lie. "I don't know how to open the fuckin' gun. That's why I didn't notice one empty." He turned slightly. "Appreciate you trying to hook us up an' that, but I really need to go. I don't feel good."

Noel was looking at Richie like he was all ready to bring the car round front and shove him in the boot. Goose paused, then said, "Go on. Go home. See your bird or whatever."

"Could be a bloke," said Noel. "You never know. Al might've turned him."

"Only thing Al ever turned was a fuckin' stomach. Go on, son."

Richie turned back to the front door. He fumbled with the latch, then stepped out into the front yard. The door closed behind him, but he could still hear Goose saying, "That little fucker left a big red smear on the wall."

It was even colder now than it was before, the wind like a slap to the face, reaching under his hoodie and biting like snakes. He started walking to the end of the path. Looked behind him to make sure nobody was watching him as he leaned on the gate, shuffled through. Then he continued up the street, walked until Goose's house was out of sight, and pulled out the mobile. Goose hadn't asked for it back. Probably forgot.

Richie was pretty sure there were minutes left on the phone. Not that he really needed them for the call he was about to make — it was a Freephone number.

He didn't call the police. They tape all their calls. Plus, they always wanted to know who it was on the other end of the line. There was never any privacy with the polis. They were all about names.

Which was why he was pressing the fives and ones. Getting through to Crimestoppers.

He waited for the line to pick up, then he said, "There was a shooting on the Leam. The Leam Lane estate. Outside The Admiral. This afternoon. The gun's with a gadgie I know. I reckon him or one of his mates might've had something to do with it."

When Richie was asked for an address, he gave it. Then he hung up, carried on down the street and chucked the mobile into the first bin that hadn't been torn off its post.

He kept walking, the blood going out of his legs. The energy too. So when he saw a bench up ahead, he eased onto it. Let his head roll back and he looked up at the sky. He thought about Becka and the baby. He thought about Goose and Noel and the police.

Then he watched the stars until they disappeared to black.